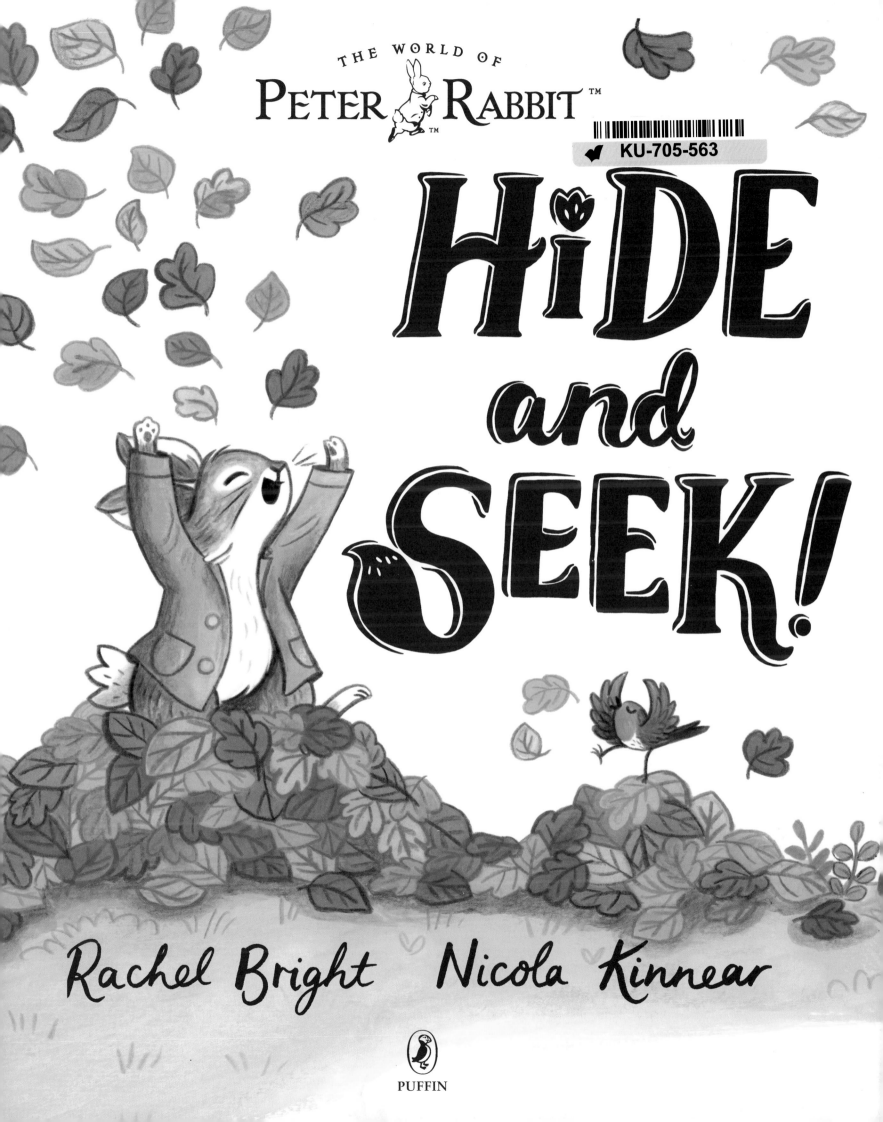

THE WORLD OF
PETER RABBIT™

HiDE and SEEK!

Rachel Bright   Nicola Kinnear

PUFFIN

Once upon a hillside,

blew a brisk autumnal breeze.

And a fellow, quite amazing,

lived below those dancing leaves.

If you look quite closely,

I think you'll see him too . . .

Two ears, some twitching whiskers

and a flash of something blue . . .

This is **PETER RABBIT!**
He is handsome, young and smart.
He is also **rather** clever,
which is where this story starts.

He was holding up a drawing
of his latest **BIG** idea!
When a shadow at the window,
very **suddenly** appeared . . .

A **RAT-A-TAT** upon it,
made him jump out of his skin!
It was his cousin Benjamin.

'PETER! LET...ME...IN!'

Benjamin climbed nimbly in,
stifling a shriek.

'Mr Tod . . . the fox!' he puffed,
'is playing **HIDE**-and-**SEEK!**'

'He asked me,' whispered Benjamin,
'to join his favourite game.'

'But,' he added with a gulp,
'**DINNER** was his aim!'

Then a tiny moment later
they heard a teeny yelp.
And Timmie Willie dived in too!
'Hide me, Peter! **HELP!**'

Timmy had been chased
by Mr Tod **as well** that day.
'Thank goodness,' shuddered Peter,
'you were quick and got away!'

Peter's lightning brain
was working nineteen to the dozen
on how to stop his friends
from ending up in old Tod's oven!

'*I'VE GOT IT!*' shouted Peter,
and he grabbed his book in glee.
'We'll outfox Mr Tod this time!
Just you wait and see!'

'We'll gather up the fallen leaves
from all around the oak,
to make ourselves a *rather fine*...

Benjamin and Timmy
danced in circles of surprise.
'Why, Peter, you're a genius!
Let's make it **NOW!**' they cried.

'My cousin is a tailor mouse!
He taught me how to sew!
I can clip and stitch and snip and fit
and show you what I know.'

They worked all through the morning
until the cloak was done.
'*Now*' winked Peter Rabbit,
'hide-and-seek will be more **FUN!**'

Peter put the cloak on,
with a vow to test it out.
'This will fool old Mr Tod!
Of **THAT** there is no doubt!'

And Peter started prancing!
'I look dashing!' he was humming.
'Peter!' whispered Benjamin . . .

. . . Mr Tod **IS COMING!**

'Watch this!' said Peter cheekily,
and to his friends' dismay,
called 'Yoo-hoo, Mr Toddy-Tod!
Hide-and-seek's **THIS WAY!**'

Mr Tod slunk over,
fixing Peter with a stare.
'Very well . . . I'll count to ten,
then see if anybody's there!

O . . . n . . . e . . . and *two* . . . and skip a few,
Haha . . . let's skip the lot!
I'm *coming* now to find you
if you're ready or you're not!'

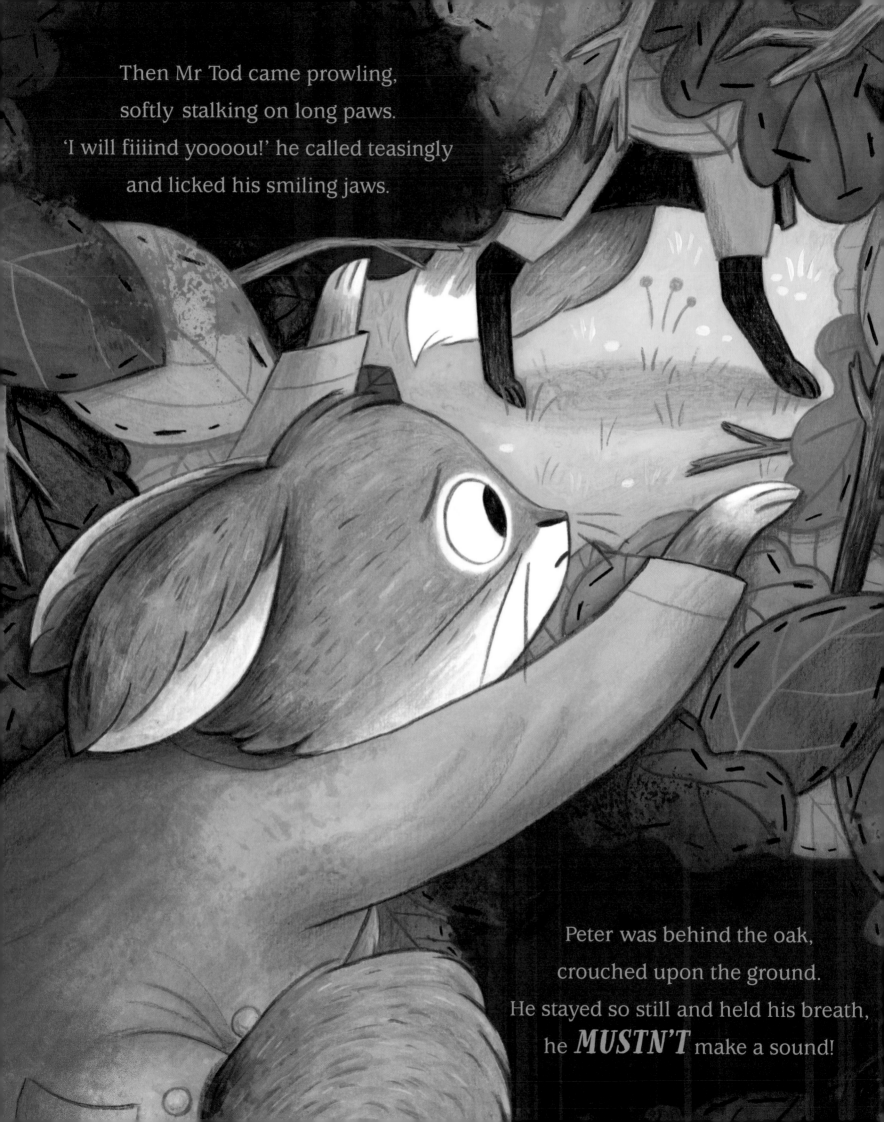

Then Mr Tod came prowling,
softly stalking on long paws.
'I will fiiiind yoooou!' he called teasingly
and licked his smiling jaws.

Peter was behind the oak,
crouched upon the ground.
He stayed so still and held his breath,
he **MUSTN'T** make a sound!

As Mr Tod approached him,
Peter used his cloaky tricks!
So all that Mr Tod could see
was piles of leaves and sticks!

And right on past he trotted!
Then away on foxy feet.
The coast was clear and Peter's cloak
had worked a perfect treat!

Mr Tod had wanted Peter's friends
to **GOBBLE** up for tea!
But they'd fooled him with the cloak
and now the three were really free!

Peter was a hero!
His plan had really worked.
But while they celebrated,
Mr Tod . . . well . . .

HE still lurked . . .

Since although he hadn't *seen* them,
he'd heard their whoops and cheering,
and he'd slunk back to the tree
to **HIDE** and plan a reappearing!

SUDDENLY he pounced upon the unsuspecting Peter, missing his white fluffy tail by just a millimetre!

The three jumped up like lightning!
They scarpered and they scattered.
Escaping from this hungry fox
was all that really mattered!

Peter ran for all his life,
he **had** to get away.

He'd had **ENOUGH**

of hide-and-seek . . .
He didn't want to play!

Then Peter saw his window!
And hopped in with a twist.
Mr Tod . . . he leapt as well . . .

. . . but *luckily*
he **MISSED!**

And Peter told his mama
all about the hide-and-seek
while she wrapped him in her arms
and placed a kiss upon his cheek.

'Oh, Peter,' she said softly,
'that's a lesson not to boast!
Come and warm your paws
and have some calming jam on toast.'

That evening Peter feasted
by the fire all safe and snug.
Pledging that **NEXT** time he'd
not be know-it-all or smug!

And Benjamin and Timmy
were home all safe and cosy too.

(And Mr Tod?
Well, he made do
with roasted-acorn stew.)

Tomorrow was another day.
Who knew what it might bring?
Certainly a chance to build
an even **BETTER** thing!

He'd think up new inventions and
of course, he would endeavour
to **NEVER** get so proud again,
and be a bit *more* clever!

Goodnight, Peter Rabbit,
we'll let you dream away,
and see you on the hillside
another wild, free day.

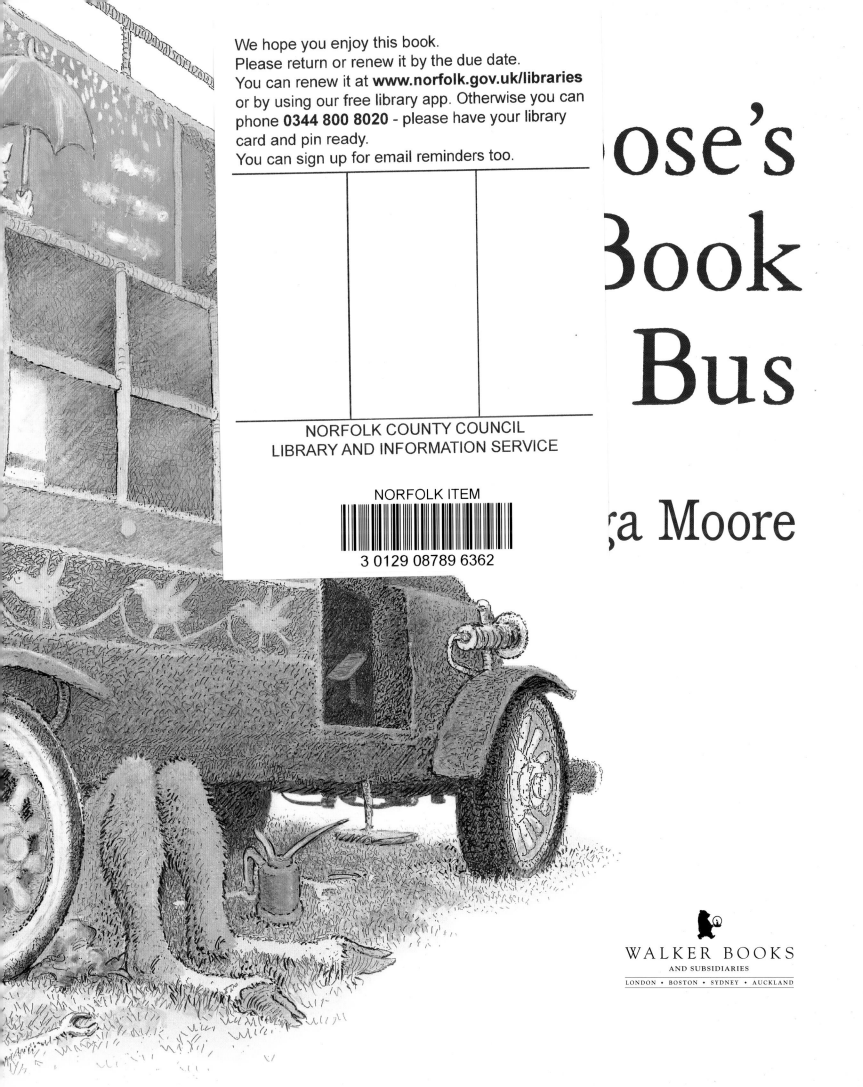

ose's
Book
Bus

ga Moore

WALKER BOOKS
AND SUBSIDIARIES
LONDON · BOSTON · SYDNEY · AUCKLAND